PARADOXICAL

THE STORY OF ANU AND AADI

ARUN D I

to Anu & Aadi

Contents

Author

Arun is a scientist, artist, story teller and a traveller.

Preface

She had a nightmare, which made her travel back in time to save him,

While going, she accidentally knocked down the lantern that took him away from her forever,

...paradoxically !

Acknowledgements

Thanks,

to parents for letting me experience life,

to my sister for bothering to get me company,

to my friends for trusting me,

to those memories for helping me to wander in the realms of unlimited imagination,

to my little boy Aarav for new experiences.

Prologue

The ambulance van caught speed with mild quiver. It is chilly inside and a lot of life saving instruments is hung all around. The windscreen barriers prevented any light from outside. Two of the medical assistants inside are trying hard to keep her conscious, as the severe blood loss and the shock of the event slumps her eyelids again and again, even when she tried to keep them open.

Her lips moved slowly trying to spell the name 'Aadi', but it died down between her stiffened jaws.

One of the ambulance staff is pressing the oxygen mask on to her face, monitoring the vitals, as Anu swigs the words, which her mind want to speak out, down her blood painted throat. She's weak and deadened on what just happened. The chaotic din at the accident spot faded into the strident noise of the emergency honk of the vehicle. A stream of blood ran down her temple from between her otherwise drenched, frenzied hair and it joined the tears across her right eyes. The ambulance staff is wiping and cleaning the blood with a piece of cotton and reassuring her.

Anu felt the brightness inside the closed van growing gradually and the surroundings are getting dissolved into it. Strapped on to the stretcher, as she was slowly falling into a stupor, her left hand fingers felt a familiar touch.

Aadi!

Her pupils dilated, and mind spontaneously concluded it as Aadi.

He's here. . . !

Her breathing got faster, tears flooded eyes as she turned her head slowly to her left to see Aadi sitting next to her. No blood, no bruise. Smiling like yesterday evening at the dungeon. His fists tightened around her palm. She does not want to believe that her mind is tricking on her.

Minutes before she saw Aadi being pulled out from his car dowsed with blood, motionless.

The brightness spreads faster now, as she felt the tightness of Aadi's fists on her, but confused on the predetermination paradox that happened a few minutes ago.

Anu pressed her underbelly with her right hand, where grows their epitome of love.

Tears rolled down her cheeks as she slowly closed eyes in anguish.

CHAPTER I

The room is dim lit with the yellow light from the bedside lamp. The air conditioner fan blows chilling air down from the right side wall. Anjali and Shivani, the little kids lying on either sides of Anu, are peacefully asleep. Anu's sweaty forehead and uneven breathing echoed about some panicky dreams which she was going through then. Her left hand fist clenches the chest side of her shirt which she was wearing, in panic.

Φ

People are rushing calling out loudly in panic "Accident!"

It was when she crossed the median line and hit another heading vehicle.

The clamant, followed by dead silence, and both the vehicles flew apart of which one toppled on the impact.

A huge jolt shook the road and died slowly into silence with time. It was less crowded though.

Anu found her face pressing on to the steering wheel with blood dripping from her face on to her lap, after her car made few circles on colliding. A sudden numbness spread all over the body.

She's being carried by few people in a stretcher, as pain has numbed her body and blood flows down from her forehead blinds everything around. Any noise is vaguely heard as her ears are still ringing much loudly unpleasantly.

As they pulled her out of the car, she sees a familiar face, 'Aadi', wearing a blood tinted white t-shirt and lying half way out of the windscreen.

He's drenched in blood and was felt helpless. His face was painted red with blood, arms hung down seemingly boneless as they lifted him out. His white t-shirt has blood strokes with different intensities. Blood drips from his body while people make him lie down on the road. Someone was shaking him and trying to wake him up. Aadi turns his face in pain and Anu sees him looking at her.

Blood from her eyebrows makes everything blurred, but she's unable to wipe them. She's being carried by few people in a stretcher.

A sudden din of the closing of the ambulance door made her open eyes.

Φ

She woke up. It was a dream!

Anu wakes up suddenly with a gasp, sweat drips down her forehead. Heart beats at double the rate than normal. She spells the name Aadi as she's panting heavily. Some heavy banging noise is reverberating in her head.

She's under panic attack, unable to move limbs as in sleep paralysis. Her shirt is drenched in sweat.

Slowly, the noise in her head died off to the sound of air blown down from the AC unit, with the bird chirpings outside.

Wiping the sweat off her face, she turns to see her kids Anjali and Shivani.

Trying to regain conscience, she panned the room and slowly closed her eyes. Anu could clearly hear the clock ticking and the breathing of Anjali and Shivani in rhythm. Her pupils located the clock which read time as 4.45 AM. As she blinked, the dream flashed once again.

Anu could not connect anything as the dream seemed to be incomplete. She remembered those childhood mornings when she used to lie back on to bad to complete a dream. But those were pleasant ones. This is not only unpleasant, but has shown loss of life also.

Anu, lying on her back, looking up the blank ceiling, was in pain. She felt severe congestion somewhere between her throat and nose which was not easing as any other time.

She's in pain.

CHAPTER II

Anu was short in breath. She crawled down from bed and walked to the washroom. Even while standing in front of the mirror, she was fully pre-occupied with the scenes in the nightmare. She saw the sweat drenched shirt which belonged to Aadi. She remembered the last time she visited him at his place.

Anu washed her face and noticed the glimmering white diamond in the nose pin which shined brighter than yesterday evening. Water dripped down her eyes and eyebrows following the contours of her face.

Among the frontal hair above forehead the reddish tinge caught her eye, which was the leftover of the vermilion. Anu's eyes weighed heavy on this as memories, both good and bad, passed by.

She sighed and it created a misty cloud on the mirror in front of her which faded away slowly clearing reality once again. She saw Anushna, 28 years old married woman and mother of two girls.

Anu's eyebrows rose, eyes wide open in partial disagreement with reality and she waved her head in distress.

Catching hold of the towel, she wiped her face and pressed hard to remove the reddishness of vermilion on her forehead in vain.

She unbuttoned her sweat-wet shirt and her eyes spotted, as always, the remnants of those pain marks which made her hate days and nights once. Unpleasant events of a failed marriage criss-crossed her mind as she closed eyes to escape.

The red straps of her bralette outlined the pink assault marks in her fair skin. A heavy breath parted her lips and escaped out as a sigh again.

Anu got into a maroon dress which was hung on the bathroom handle bar.

She felt that her heart continued the irregular beats and her pupils wandered in confusion, as she tried to phone Aadi multiple times. It all ended saying he's not available at the other side.

Anu exited the washroom with a decision to drive to Aadi, as he was not responding to any calls or messages from her.

Shivani, the elder one was hugging Anju, the toddler and both were fast asleep. Anu sat to the foot-side of the bed looking at the girls. She moved up her palms on to Shiva's legs staring at them blankly.

"Amma, are you fine?" Shivani's sleepy voice of concern woke Anu from a trance.

She tried to bring a mild smile to acknowledge and asked Shiva to sleep holding her sister.

Anu spotted an unread message from Arjun which stayed as an unnoticed notification.

Anything with tag of Arjun raises her heartbeat.

On clicking, it read 'I'll not let you both live peacefully'.

Ashwini's message read 'Hello dear, how are you, how are kiddos?'. Anu felt sorry for her as she had missed a few calls on previous day from Ashwini and could not call back. But then, Anu knew no emotions other than anxiety.

She went back to the dialler and attempted calling Aadi once again, and it ended again without response.

Her fingers moved the phone screen to the photo gallery where images of Anju and Shiva occupied most of the folders, but one. Aadi was having a place in the gallery where those images sent by him, for him and with him are stored. This was the one Arjun tried and failed to open as he couldn't guess the folder password. In fact Anu was clever enough to keep the password as 'Arjun' as that was the least expected one he would attempt to open. As an extension to this thought, came to mind the tortures she had to bear as Arjun failed to guess the password.

No calls or responses yet.

Anu stood up and walked close to Anjali and kissed on both of their foreheads and patted them with motherly care.

She walked away from the bed and reached for the door. Descending the stairs, Anu walked to her parent's room. As she reached near, Mom opened the door and asked her what had happened as she found Anu ready for leaving the house during those early hours.

Anu hugged her mom and replied "Go to the kids mummy, I'm going to check whether Aadi's safe. I've had a very bad dream."

Obstinate, as always, mom replied to this with a sharp face and a series of questions,

"Anu, what's your problem? Every time Aadi?!, Remember you're a married woman and mother of two children. Are you not bothered about their future ?, Don't you have anything left for Arjun, your husband ?, How many times we will try to make you understand these things ?, At least consider your age old parents and give us a peaceful death !. You know, your dad has not slept since he heard about your broken marriage. Why can't you adjust with Arjun and continue life? Anju and Shiva at least will have their biological father."

Staring at her silently, Anu held her shoulders as if indirectly asking her to stop questioning.

"If you cannot help me, please try to understand me at least! I cannot live with Arjun anymore. Past eight years I was suffering alone. My kids know about it, and I do not want them to settle for this. They deserve better life. I deserve better life. I do not understand yet that why my parents alone can't get it".

Anu took a pause after stressing the last sentence, and continued with eyes lowered slowly.

"I have adjusted since long for not breaking hearts of you people. Now I realize I too have a heart. I love Aadi and I'm sure that he'll be the best father for my children. And obviously, better than the so called biological father!"

Knowing the stubborn character of Anu, mom who lost hope of convincing her, nodded in disagreement.

Keeping her left palm on her underbelly, Anu continued "I'm having his child in me and we are going to bring it up with Shiva and Anju as Aadi wished. We will live peacefully and happily. Please try to understand."

Anu witnessed emotions of mom leaping from sadness to deeper sadness obviously... Mom started crying as Anu held her arms tight for few seconds and then walked away picking the car keys. Anu wiped tears from her left cheek with the back of her left hand as she opened the main door.

She could hear her dad asking something to Mom, but her priority made her pull away the gate and get inside the car.

Her dad, who had always listened to her stories, stood at the door as she drove the car past the gate. He was silent and emotionless. Anu remembered about her dad's dead silence right from her childhood, whenever his words would have given strength to face the music ringing across the corners of life.

Φ

Father is the girl child's first love and his care and affection slowly moulds her thoughts and concepts about a partner in future.

Φ

Silence at wrong time makes one undeserving to voice at some right time.

As she shifted to top gear, Anu remembered about the childhood days when she used be dear to dad, before he left to Abu Dhabi for work.

CHAPTER III

Anu's heartbeat still followed some irregular pattern but mind was wandering in search of thoughts to sooth her and ease her worries. A bicycle rider crossed the road right in front of her as Anu was waiting at the red signal.

Suddenly she felt the daylight brightening, the traffic signal post turning to a banyan tree with branches growing to all sides, and everything appeared to be familiar.

Her mind dug the memories out of all possible folds in her brain. She is seeing the school boy Aadi pushing his bicycle and walking down the road to the tuition centre, silently smiling and intermittently humming a song. He was a lean boy wearing a white half sleeve shirt tucked in his steel grey uniform pants. Oily hair was combed up revealing his wide forehead and thick eyebrows. He had light stubbles adoring his fair cheeks, still revealing dimples on smiles. Hanging a side bag to his left shoulder he resembled a poet of some old era. The royal blue bars of the cycle too appeared to be from an old generation. Those oval spectacle frame on his nose added charm to his composed looks.

Anu smiled at this flash of memory.

The vehicle behind her honked continuously, on the shift of the signal light to green and she pushed the gear and moved the car, while her thoughts chose to stay at the same nostalgic layer of life.

Φ

The classroom had only three or four students all studying in grade ten. Most of them knew each other from childhood and shared the same locality. Pooja and Rejisha were sitting in the front row busy noting down the lecture while Nishad was in second row with a vacant seat beside him. Then the lean guy in white shirt is sitting in last row, swirling a pen between his long lean fingers in right hand.

It was Mr.Vinay's chemistry class where IUPAC names where discussed and everyone welcomed this new girl with smiles except the last bench lean guy. He was peeking through the space above his spectacles with serious face.

The navy blue colour long skirt and white shirt imparted an air of mystery around her. He peered those the bright eyes bordered with thick layers of eye-liner and the curious looks in them. The long raven black hair braided on two sides gave her the typical village girl look and the calmness and silence added on to the conundrum that surrounded her. The bright silver anklets and black glass bangles sought his attention with the tinkling sound as she entered the classroom.

"He's Aadityan, this is Pooja, Rejisha and myself Nishad"

Nishad enthusiastically introduced everyone, as Mr.Vinay was busy talking to Anu's father. Both the girls nodded and smiled at her and Nishad was stretching out his right hand for a handshake with a big smile. Aadityan, on this, stretched his closed lips for a moment giving her the feel of a formal smile, and then looked down.

Everyone except Aadityan took note of the lectures while he used to sit looking at the text book swirling the pen and rocking his body, and always chose to sit in the last row. As the lecture progressed Mr.Vinay stopped and said "Yes Aadi, now what's it". Everyone turned to the last row to see Aadi's right hand raised while he was writing something with his left hand on the margin space of his text book.

"Can you come again please, that was not clear?"

That was the first time Anu heard Aadi, that too after seven days of attending the same class. He had a soft transforming voice that of the teenager, somewhere between a sturdy male and a boy child.

Slowly the group turned into a bunch of good friends. All of them talked about fun moments in their schools, shared snacks while waiting for the lecturer, walked back home after the classes together. Pooja and Rejisha used to come first in class, but Aadityan knew many things beyond text book also, Nishad used to be good in solving numerical and Anu had to struggle to match with the group. Aadi used to ask questions to Mr.Vinay and keep the class fun filled. The examples Aadi uses to explain his questions used to be very comprehensive and hence all of them including Mr.Vinay enjoyed the class.

Everyone used to borrow Aadi's textbooks as he's got information beyond the scope of the syllabus even, scribbled on the margins of the book. He was focused and went behind everything which struck his curiosity. Others admired him, but for Anu it walked past admiration to adoration slowly. She shifted to the last row at times, which left Nishad give jealous looks. On finish of classes Anu's father used to wait to pick her back home and her eyes pan to bid adieu to Aadi. They spoke little but those looks communicated much more than words.

Φ

Anu pulled up the windscreen and set the wiper turned on as it suddenly started to drizzle. The vehicles on the road slowed down due to steady strengthening of rain. It was 5.10 AM as Anu looked at the phone screen. She attempted calling Aadi once again, which was unanswered as earlier. Her panicky mind started filling her mind with unwelcome thoughts. She shook her head and sighed heavily holding the steering wheel tighter. Trying to move out of the packed traffic, she honked few times.

Φ

It was raining that evening and Anu did not have an umbrella. Pooja and Rejisha had their fathers waiting to pick them with rain coats and Nishad did not turn up that day. As Mr.Vinay was locking the class room, Aadi told Anu "Come, I shall drop you. I have an umbrella".

Anu, blushed and agreed at once and they both started walking back home. Aadi seemingly walked slowly as if silently they had an agreement. No words uttered, but Anu could hear her heartbeat in excitement. She was trying hard to hide her smile at times whenever she felt the umbrella is small enough for two people. She realised Aadi too was holding back his smiles in excitement at times.

The eyes of the little girl sparkled like those of angels.... Something that he adored the most.... he always looked at them in oblivion...and never disrupted the calmness that prevailed around her.... he felt as if they were two magic balls that hid themselves inside the krubera caves sealed with a thick layer of kajal. Whenever he looked at them he felt as if he was going in anonymity. Once he tried to tell her what he felt when she was around, but she ran away out of fear.... She was an angel... she used to look at him as well but was too scared to tell him what she felt for him.

"It was just a drizzle. You could have walked home without umbrella even" An unexpected manly voice stopped both of them. Anu's father appeared in front of them in his bike. Yes the heavy rain has died down to just a drizzle, which they failed to realize. Anu silently sat pillion to dad, while the folds in his forehead revealed that he was annoyed on the event. The same folds appeared the next day while she was caught walking back home with Aadi as Mr.Vinay did not turn up. Again few more times, those forehead folds made Anu stop the tuition.

Later Aadi was caught few times tightening the bicycle chain in and around Anu's house premises in attempts to see her.

Φ

Thoughts about Aadi were jumping back to mind even when she was looking to overtake the vehicle in front.

A text message appeared on Anu's phone which suddenly pulled her back from the nostalgic trance.

No relief, more pain. It's Arjun.

"Happy anniversary my dear wife, don't ever even dream of leaving me. I shall hunt you down wherever you live"

A flash of the past eight years went past in front of her eyes in a blink.

Φ

She was about three when her Dad left to Abu Dhabi, moments of which Anu hardly remembers. Growing up was hard at times as she envied many of her school mates being dropped by their fathers when she alight the school van. Now after few days of dropping for school and tuitions, when her dad felt uneasy watching his daughter being followed by a guy, he moved the entire family to Abu Dhabi. It was without any prior notice to any of the family member. This she discovered when she found her elder brother revolting against father's plans, as it destroyed the idea of joining college with his friends.

Anu and Aadi parted.

She cried for days, but of no use.

Aadi continued the bicycle chain tightening idea in front Anu's house for some more days without knowing she was relocated to a far place. Slowly he realized that she's not anymore available to peep through the curtains and smile.

CHAPTER IV

It's 5.20 AM on the clock tower which Anu drove past and no reply messages or calls yet. And the intensity of rain steadily increased.

Φ

Mother wanted to come back to hometown after two years of Abu Dhabi life, and that dictated Anu's life too. She just finished her twelfth class in Global Indian International School and now being relocated again to India.

Father's kinship with some renowned politician helped to secure a seat for Anu in a famous all girls' college in the city. As father's plans were driven only by the situations, no one in family will have the privilege to choose as per their will.

Anu was admitted for bachelors in English literature.

She was an average student in her school, but subsequently some climate changes played good and the international experience made her excel in her degree course. She came top among her counterparts in the university, even though this achievement did not amaze others in her family.

Φ

She's standing at the main gate of the most distinguished college of the state as her classmates pulled her where the inter-collegiate fest was all set to rock the stage. It's the world of youth, men women and couples.

After the official inaugural ceremony the students and spectators moved to the open amphi-theatre where the cultural events were about to start.

Stalk and stares were not new though, but one pair of eyes following them amused Anu and her friends. A stout gentleman in a skin tight t-shirt and blue textured jeans was interested in the gang even when the music was played in loudest possible volume from the stage. Anu was trying to recollect the face which felt familiar.

"That's Arjun. He was my neighbour once. He had a soft feeling towards me which I rejected during tenth grade itself"

Anu whispered to her friends nearby.

The figure disappeared from there then and appeared suddenly in front of Anu. She got startled, but boldly looked at him. On introducing to her friends, he sought few minutes to talk to Anu away from the crowd.

Again he proposed her for marrying him right away referring to their last meeting and her last rejection, this time quoting the achievement of completing Engineering in some strange named College. Anu was nervous but remained content. Arjun smiled at Anu who reciprocated by looking at her watch.

"I have given my reply once to you Arjun, and that remains same now also"

Arjun did not seem annoyed by this as he smiled fixing eyes to some distant views and silently looked at her when she walked back to her friends.

Φ

The resplendent marriage was celebrated in a grandiose manner. The huge hall had an elaborate decoration with white jasmine flowers with a big Ganesha in the middle; the destroyer of all obstacles. The decorated dais pavilion of the hall was highlighted with aster flowers and red roses. The aisle which leads to the dais was embellished on both sides

with flowers and lighted brass lamps. With the rise in beat of the thavil and nadaswaram, the bride was blushing as she had been brought to the mandap by her proud father. All eyes were focusing on the princess and her poise. The groom gave a glance at his bride who was red in face and couldn't restrain herself from reciprocating. The gold jewellery covering her upper body to adorn her made her look like a mannequin in a display cabinet. But her smile was more than enough to rob the hearts of those who assembled there.

Arjun married Anushna !

The bride entered the vintage car decorated with festoons of marigold and chrysanthemum. Her dream of sitting alongside her man was pushed to the backseat of the car along with her in laws. The mehendi in her hands told a thousand tales though a little bit dull now. The blazing afternoon sun was trying to bake her dreams but the desire inside her was too strong that even sun couldn't lessen it. The car was moving really fast just like the reverie of the beautiful girl. It seemed to her as if she was getting closer to the greatest days of her life.

CHAPTER V

Rain stopped and splodges of stagnant water reminded her of the roads to paternal grandmother's house visits during teenage. One of such visit gifted her stardom of women hood for which her parents came down to fete her on the new beginning. But whenever she wished their presence, they never appeared.

Φ

"What the hell have you been doing all day here... look at the room. What a mess it is..."Anu was aroused from her sleep, her babies sleeping close to her clinging on to their mother. She got up in a hurry looked around the messy room. The drowsy eyes couldn't be opened completely but managed to do so. She cleaned up the floor in a hurry, cleared the bed. Arjun had been at office till 9 in the evening, he was having a video conference with his client abroad and that's why he came so late. It's true that he had been working hard all day, but she too was not relaxing.

Anu hurried down the stairs to the kitchen.

Arjun's mother was preparing food for dinner.

"Amma, sorry I fell asleep..."Anu said in a blameworthy tone.

"It's okay Anu, come and have some food. You didn't take anything since noon"

Anu smiled as reply to her as she was walking and muttering.

She is a silly goose, living to take care of the demands of the big family, managing them for more than thirty years. Yet she seems so happy and never tired of anything. But behind her smiling face Anu knows very clearly that she had been wearing a mask of content before the world.

As a woman she had no choice. And many a times she tried to take her out of the self-imposed cage, but failed terribly. She was too scared of the world, the people around her, but was obsessed with the "looking good" feeling. But she never realized the fact that she had been losing herself all these years.

"Oh, you already had your dinner... girls these days don't even have the demeanour of waiting till their husbands have food..." said Kokila aunty. Kokila is Arjun's aunt staying at Mumbai, a polished sophisticated lady with an atrocious attitude. She observes everything very carefully and manipulates everything in the family. Though married to a well-known family, she has broken ties with them and is now at her maternal home along with her children and grandchildren. Seeing Anu and her mother in law sharing a cordial relationship Kokila feels badly disturbed and will never lose an opportunity to create an uncertainty in the peaceful co-existence.

"No aunty, Arjun already had his dinner... that's why..."

Arjun's mother gets influenced with surroundings faster than anyone. She can be manipulated with that influence. Hearing Kokila, she did not respond or defend Anu.

"You don't have to give me an explanation..." she interrupted Anu without letting her complete the sentence.

"By the way, why do you let him have food outside... these are all problems you know, don't you know that all these are not good for Arjun's health? Can't you prepare tasty dishes at home? This is the reason why he hates eating from home... they are all the same... these new girls who want to work... become independent...earn money... they don't have time for anything... even look at the kids... how lean they are...our kids used to be really plump and chubby at this age... right Valyamma?"

Valyamma, the maternal grandmother had been taking care of the family for the past fifty years. She was widowed at a very young age, but as an embodiment of strength and will power, she fought with the entire world for her worth, her children and her life. She was a lady full of pride and self-respect. Nothing could harm her, even touch her. She was the cornerstone of the family. Her words were the decree which no one objected. She was the absolute epithet.

"You are absolutely right Kokila..."said Valyamma. "Girls these days are full of self-love and self-admiration. They are not bothered about anything else and having the feeling that they know everything"

Valyamma looked at Anu with resentment in her eyes. Anu got up from the chair with the plate in her hands, two driblets of warm water made her eyes moist. By almost 10:30, she finished her chores and went to sleep. Arjun was there, waiting for her.

The entire act took almost 5 -7 minutes and Arjun turned to the other side to steer clear off from Anu. She lay there like a worn piece of cloth and after sometime got up and went to the wash room.

Cleansing herself off the unwanted particles that greased her body she came back to see Shivani sitting up on bed and was crying.

"What happened baby?" Anu asked.

She was snivelling and couldn't talk. On having water which Anu gave, Shiva asked her in low voice. "Why did Dad knock you down Mom?" Anu was not shocked with the question as she knew very well that Shivani was growing up fast and could understand all these very soon. Anu consoled her and switched off the lights, went to bed.

Weird thoughts shoved into her memory lane without asking permission and took away sleep from her eyes.

Though Anu tried to sleep, she couldn't revert herself from the cogitation.

She was able to see the newly married woman entering her marital home. The antique car decorated in a showy manner with golden and yellow chrysanthemums stopped right in front of the big gate. The walkway was also decorated with flowers to welcome her. The big mansion, the fleet of cars that greeted her, added colour to her dreams of a perfect life.

"Dear, you won't be worrying about anything there... they are good people and Arjun will look after you better than anyone else..." her mother's words resonated in her ears. After the traditional nuptial ceremonies she got ready for the reception that evening.

Relatives and friends came in great numbers to the house greeting the couple long life and a healthy relationship. Anu glanced at Arjun every now and then expecting a smile from him in return, but was feeling dejected with his cold reaction. It was too late when the house was taken back to the calmness of night. Anu went early to her new room. Just as she had seen in some Bollywood movies, she expected her room to be prepared well for their first night and the over-dressed sister in law taking her to the room cracking some slimy joke with a glass of milk in her hands. But she failed to experience anything like that. Her sister in law was fast asleep and all other rooms were overloaded with the din of snoring.

Anu entered her room or rather the bedroom which is going to be her now on.

It was good even though not decorated as per her desire. She tried to change her clothes and searched for the new ones. But there was nothing in the wardrobe except Arjun's old clothes. Not even a single one. Anu stood there not knowing what to do.

After almost half an hour Arjun came. Her eyes flashed a streak of bashfulness. She couldn't look into his eyes. The anxiety, embarrassment and delight altogether reddened her. She stood up from bed looking down at the floor. The dim lighting added on to the feel.

"Anu, you have not changed yet?" asked Arjun, switching on few more lights. Anu remained startled at the sudden reaction of her husband.

"I... don't have anything to change that's why...." She tried to explain.

"Will you please get me my suitcase from the other room?" she asked.

"No need for changing at this time... come let's go to bed."

The anxiety slowly gave way to scare. She slowly moved towards Arjun... lights went off. She could still feel the pain penetrating into the bride's body.

Φ

Anu trembled out of her evocation. The memories made her weak. But she was very clear about what to do next. The pain, the agony, the feeling of being exploited made her fume with rage. But she had to preserve it from exploding. Only then she will be able to utilize it against the fate which brought her to this condition. She is not against anything. Not against anyone. She just wanted to ease her difficulties, wanted to be free of worries like any other wife and mother, live a happy life.

The brahminy kite flew high above the sky. A white dove around its neck was seen flying freely under the kite

fearlessly. The dove spread its wings and flew relaxed manner. It seemed as if the kite was protecting the dove. The symbiotic relation of the two birds couldn't be explained by anyone. One was the angel and the other was human. But at times both resided in the birds equally, making it difficult for the spectators to identify who's who.

Φ

Transformation of Arjun had been drastic and happened in a short duration beyond the honeymoon period. All the male names in Anu's phone were doubted as her lovers. Any chats made by her should be shown to Arjun whenever asked. Any words to her mother or father, describing her difficulty were treated as treachery against Arjun and would be punished.

Anu's dream family life was blown away even while she did multiple attempts to hold them together. Arjun, the dictator turned her parents against Anu revealing even those manipulated bedroom conversations. If she spells out any difficulty, the same were branded as lie and betrayal. She became helpless. Kids became her only hope to traverse through the day.

Never did Anu feel her and kids prioritized ahead of his parents, as she suffered insults time and again by Arjun in front of her in laws.

Most of the daily routine starts with Arjun waking up Anu for quenching his bodily needs early morning, even while the kids are on same bed. Pulling down her dress, he straight away enters her till he drains himself, and the act never lasted more than few minutes and he was never bothered about her feelings and needs as a partner. She remained undone and unsatisfied even while he gets exhausted in the act.

After noon, once he returns from office, the act repeats even ignoring presence of kids, as he prioritizes his lust and pleasures above all. Questioning, showing unhappiness or dissatisfaction would result in assaulting which even once left Anu with a fractured right hand pinkie finger. Once, on self defence she had to push him away which was put in front of in laws as unbecoming a wife.

So, she never complained then on. Sufferings were covered up.

As he found her forgetting to smile and behave emotionless, the torture took a turn to another level where a new person was brought in, a Psychiatrist.

...the night then was darker and was scarier than any other. The howling of the cold wind through the woods gave an eerie ambience to the old house. The girl was sitting in front of the bookrack skimming through the untitled manuscripts. She was very enthusiastic to find out the rest of the bit she found outside the building. But instead of the missing page what she found was a picture of a fawn being chased by a hound. Just as she was wondering at the mural she could feel the warm hands of the stranger on her waist. Her husband, who became a stranger by now, whose presence, scared the fawn, the girl.

Φ

It was 5.40 AM and Anu remembered that it was September 04 that day and nine years since she is a married woman.

She checked phone for any reply messages or calls.

Found nothing.

Φ

Anniversaries after the first one has always been predictable and one sided.

Every time she cooked for Arjun and waited till late night. He returned home after partying with friends or meetings at office. Sometimes on reminding, he might wish her and show a repenting face for not gifting her anything. But that is forgotten in no time.

Eighth wedding anniversary coincided with one of Arjun's friend's marriage. The evening reception party happened to be in the ball-room of one of the finest hotels in the city, for which Arjun asked Anu and kids to get ready. It was an unusual experience for Anu as he never liked her to be presented anywhere. He blames the beautiful face of his wife for not being taken anywhere outside, and the justification has been 'To avoid staring and stalking'.

Arjun was never the kind of a person who loved silence of nature and that too at night; he only loved to make people silent. Arjun was a scaredy-cat, so unlike his appearance. He was scared of almost everything in his life... night...darkness...death...diseases and everything around him. He was even scared of taking his wife to public.

No different from any other day, the journey was full of arguments and fights. This time it was for kids stepping on the newly changed leather seats of his brand new Audi Q7. Arjun never liked the usage 'Our car' by anyone, Anu remembered. For him, it was 'his car' and others whoever it is, are just passengers.

The reception hall was nearly forty minutes away from their home. Anjali and Shivani were excited, but sat quiet in fear of Arjun's wrath which is unpredictable for any questions or comments.

Just few minutes before the hotel entrance road, a public work road blockage made them slowdown. Anu was candidly looking outside fixing her eyes on the vague reflection from the windscreen. Her pupils followed the moving objects and suddenly caught some familiar face beside a dozer parked by the roadside.

Her mind suddenly felt some chillness and a brisk of emotions bubbled out.

'Aadi!' Anu's lips silently spelled.

Long after thirteen years, she had a glimpse of the face. With beard and spectacles, he's grown as a man, but she recognized him.

Has he noticed her? Anu was still in the excitement, even while they've parked the car inside the hotel premise. Arjun again shouted at Anu for not obeying his orders, which she did not even listen.

She spent the next one hour in the hotel, meeting the newlywed couple and taking dinner with kids, following orders from Arjun, all mechanically with a pre-occupied mind.

Aadi, with whom she parted after tenth grade, is seen again coincidentally. On return, Anu searched the name 'Aadityan Mohan, Aadityan M, Aadi in facebook and instagram to get disappointed for not finding a match.

Has he got married? Has he got kids? Does he still remember those old days?

Anu's mind wandered around Aadi the whole night and she found it difficult to sleep.

She was holding her girls and was travelling back to the good old teenage and suddenly remembered that Rejisha, the tenth grade classmate was a neighbour to Aadi. She searched for Rejisha's profile in her friends' list and messaged her.

Anu felt hesitant initially to talk with Rejisha, as she was detached with her friends since Arjun came into life. He never liked her talking with friends or sharing her life incidents with anyone. Probably the fear of getting exposed might have made him stop her.

A day of wait with multiple checking on Rejisha's chat window built up thoughts and frustration in Anu.

After a long wait, Rejisha came online. She has relocated after marriage to Australia as her man was working there. After the initial talks asking whereabouts, with restless mind, Anu inquired about Aadi.

"So this was your primary agenda right?" Rejisha giggled with digital emoticons.

"Nope...; just asked, today I saw him on the way to a function. I do not have his contact since long. So thought to ask you about him" Anu replied.

"He finished his Engineering and went abroad for masters' and doctoral degree in Physics, his favourite subject. I remember it was at Kaiserslautern, Germany" Rejisha continued for Anu's exclamations.

"Now he's looking for some faculty positions, and yes he's in hometown these days"

Anu, with a sigh thanked Rejisha as she shared Aadi's phone number also.

She knew saving the number would harm her as well as Aadi, as Arjun regularly keep a sceptical eye on anything done by her.

So she by hearted the number, and remembered to erase chat with Rejisha.

It was 3.00 AM then, but Anu started off with 'Hello Dr.Aadi', for which she was not expecting any immediate response.

To her surprise, in another ten minutes came a reply "Anushna?"

Obviously 'true caller' might have told him it's me.

Then messages and calls took them to the immediate sunrise, and the next and the next and next.

Months, which had snail's pace, slowly transformed into a hare.

Φ

Good memories brought smiles to Anu's face even while driving in panic, yet worried about no response from her dear one.

Φ

In four months and little more, they've come closer, re-established the strength of the vintage friendship. Aadi reminded her intermittently about Anu being a married woman and his presence should not affect her normal life which only left with fitful burst of emotions.

She started sharing her actual life conditions, slowly untying the bitterness of life experiences as a wife and mother of two girls, the toxicity she face being an obedient inmate in Arjun's prison.

Anu remembered Aadi giving tips initially, that can help her to change husband to a good man and reduce the sufferings of her as well as kids.

Pointless though as she 'tried and tired' in toil, but as Aadi asked to give Arjun one last chance before she think of a separation she agreed, partially.

Φ

Almost six in the morning... the little girl was walking down the lane. The sacred hymns from the temple filled the path and the air was having the sweet smell of the freshly bloomed golden champa flowers. Few kittens sprang out of the log which lay on the roadside... a cock displaying his crimson tinted blood-red and occasionally black and blue tail and sang 'cock-a-doodle-doo' on top of the fence, the rising sun gave the little girl a golden aura and the fragrance of sandalwood and rosewater filled the air

around her. As she was walking, she cast a brief look into the apricot shaded walls of the house standing out from a green background with occasional smudging and smearing of flowers of almost all colour. Her eyes were in search of someone, but were disappointed not to find him there.

Just as she went pass the gate he came running down the stairs swiftly but failed to catch a glimpse of her.

CHAPTER VI

"Mrs. Anushna, your life seems to be very complicated. But understand one thing clearly; unless and until you try to untangle the mess inside you, nobody will be able to bring you out." The lady psychiatrist, friend of Arjun told her. "...you are good enough to understand your situation and only you can help yourself out of it. I can give you medicines to get out of this, if you insist... but let me tell you frankly, you don't need that... you are capable to tackle the situation yourself...you don't need medicines." The psychiatrist came near Anu. Patting her shoulder, she said "Don't worry dear, everyone around you is struggling, may be for different reasons, but only those who will fight back will succeed."

The doctor's words reverberated through her ears. Yes the entire world had been trying to tell her the same thing. She remembered the days which were trying to pull her down and each of those incidents and happenings that brought her up back to life. Those days which she needed that closeness, that companionship the most were the worst days for her. She recollected the first visit to the psychiatrist. After reaching home it seemed as if Arjun lost his cool completely. "How dare you wretched creature? You tried to defame my family...my reputation...you whore... I should have thrown you away that day itself, when you showed signs of insanity... worthless creature. You are here to destroy everything... all happiness and peace from my home. You will kill us all. You will destruct everything good around you. Not even a single moment..." Anu closed her eyes in pain and cried. She felt humiliated as Arjun shouted all these in front of his family. She was mortified. She felt subjugated. She couldn't hold it anymore.

"Enough.. Arjun! Enough... please stop it!" Arjun was taken aback with the sudden change in Anu. He felt demeaned before his family, but quickly reacted, "you swine!! You are talking back..."the huge hand fell on her face reddening it. But Anu too was not going to suffer anymore. She stood up and looking into his eyes she slapped him in front of the whole family. Nobody moved. Even before they could understand what was happening, Anu left the house with her children.

The dove seemed to be scared, but it had to fly. The sky seemed to be limitless and the grey sky was too petrifying, but she flew. Accumulating all strength and energy she flew above the grey clouds and dark sky, way high, touching the upper limit of the sky where she can't go higher. There she tried to sustain for a long time. And flew, maintaining the pace for a long time...till she saw the awesome azure blue colour cracking in through the dark...

Φ

As she drove past a hoarding which read FOR EVER TOGETHER featuring a couple in an advertisement of something, she remembered the day she took decision of parting with Arjun. It was when she went to Abu Dhabi with parents.

Φ

Anu sat down in the metallic chair inside the lounge of the international airport. Anjali was really cranky and Shivani was really tired to the core. The flight was delayed by one and a half hours. A whirlwind of emotions ran past down her memory lane.... She looked at herself on the locked phone screen. The girl who always wanted company, who always wanted to smile, to enjoy her life, was seen nowhere. Here, she can see a woman, who got tired of the experiences of life and planning to give it a twist, not knowing what exactly it would turn out to be.

"All passengers travelling to Dubai in Emirates flight no.G49..."Anu was awakened from the trance. She got up with little Anjali on her arms and moved to the gate announced by the flight steward along with Shivani. Anu was not missing anything, instead she was going blank. She could hear so many voices inside her. So many things were going on inside her mind evaluating her life events, whether she is doing the right thing or not. The voices however were not able to clarify all these and give her a satisfying answer. She felt as if they all are mocking at her. She could feel the pain of being torn apart and she being pulled down into a deep trench from where she could never escape.

A newlywed couple sitting by the window seat of Lufthansa...her lovely black tresses flying over his shoulders as she rests on it. Her dreams are taking her to the City of Love, Paris...the much awaited and well planned honeymoon trip. The polished smile of the airhostess seemed less attractive compared to the shy smile of the bride... Her sparkling eyes revealed a thousand dreams she is trying to make a reality with the man of her dreams...

Φ

The dry desert wind was too noisy but Anu couldn't hear anything. The dusty sandstorm inside her was noisier than the wind outside. She stood at the balcony of her apartment. The distant view of the ETISALAT tower was faded due to the dull light of the late afternoon. She remembered the happy girl who was so excited to come over to the dream city whenever she got a chance. It's been nearly thirty years since her dad came here. This is the place from where he got everything in his life; rather he gained everything in his life. This has become her second home where she found solace as she felt too busy and never got time to think about unwanted worries and troubles. But now things got into a new phase of life.

Looking down through the balcony, Anu could see Shiva and Anju playing at the park in front of their apartment. The uneven sea of buildings that lies in front seemed like the track of her life where she had to overcome all the hurdles to reach the other side. The dusky sky and peach coloured clouds added special effects to the dilemma that brewed inside her. She was wondering and concerned about two things, her kids and her life. She was bold enough for any decision, but was quite adamant about the fact that the life of her kids shouldn't be affected by any of her decision.

She was evoked from the daze by the ring on her phone. It was Arjun. Anu remained muddled for some time thinking what to do. As she went close to it, it stopped ringing. A second time it rang again. The second call...she remembered the way Arjun reacted whenever she failed to attend his call. The conceit inside her rose and she switched off the phone.

Anu got ready to go for an outing. She wanted to get out of all the unpleasant thoughts and weird notions intruding into her mind. The city tour and desert drive was a part of her deliberate effort. Anu got ready, took a taxi and started off to the city tour with her cherubs. The double-decker bus took her around the most beautiful manmade city in the desert. The beautiful buildings, structures, tallest tower and awesome gardens blooming in the sea of sand proclaimed that nothing is impossible for man. Though the sun was shining up there in the sky, the heat was not felt. The molten lava of the reality of her life was hotter than the heat produced inside the inner core of the sun. Shivani was super excited to get on the top of the double-decker but, Anjali was a little bit scared. But she too was enjoying the ride with curious eyes and never ending questions.

The scenic beauty of the huge structures or the golden sands of the Marina was not able to bring calmness to the throbbing heart. She was lost in her conviction and was not able to forget the sufferings she had experienced all through her life. The teenager who was promised a life of her choice, the woman who was given the vow of a happy life, the mother who wanted to dream for her children, all culminated in her giving her an image of a bugbear wherever she looked.

While returning, at some moment, Anu felt really disconnected with the world and walked away leaving her mom and kids perturbed in her capricious behaviour.

She walked through the grassy meadows of Al MAMZAR Park. There she could see couples spending quality time, families sharing moments of happiness and children enjoying evening with their parents. Anushna was missing her life, though she never wanted to go back to that life with Arjun, she doesn't want her babies to miss their father. She felt the confusion devouring her thoughts. She remained perplexed for a long time. Anu actually came a long way away with her kids to forget everything and bring clarity to her thoughts. But the stronger her desire to run away from them the closer she gets confronted by her problems.

Anu slowly walked along the beach adjacent to the park. The beach too was crowded. Children ran up and down playing games. A number of kites flew up making an asymmetric rainbow of many hues on the sky. Anu stood there for some time watching happy people, which reminded of the happiness once she experienced as a child.

The most beautiful days of one's life, Anu thought, was childhood, where no fears or worries overcome the excitement and happiness of the being alive with your dear ones.

A small girl was pulling and dragging her father to those luring waves. She seemed wanting to touch them but was too scared. The father was smiling at the giggling child, a proud smile of a happy father. The father who wanted his pie to overcome her fears is tempting her to come near the sea and touch the water.

Anu tried to imagine a conversation between them. The father rather tempting her by telling that underneath those waves are found 'oysters holding precious pearls' and showing the discarded oyster shells on shore.

The girl with bright curious eyes was obviously tempted, but was fighting with her fear.

Father walked to her and lifted her, holding her tight on the shallow water while she collected those shells. Those never gave her precious pearls, but something more valuable has come to her, the courage and strength of having a father who stands by.

The little girl who was hardly three or four years taught Anu one of the greatest lessons of her life.

Unless one faces the fear, it will keep coming, scaring one restraining you from real happiness.

CHAPTER VII

An old couple walking by the road side holding each other's hands brought a smile to Anu's face. She sighed and shifted gear to move away from the lane as a truck was honking heavily behind her.

Her mind was wandering somewhere in the past.

Φ

After a murky month, the entire family returned. This time Dad got farewell from his colleagues.

Even after discussing regarding the atrocities of Arjun, Anu's mother informed Arjun about the flight timings. What more she needs to get annoyed and Anu had a heavy face through the flight.

Arjun waited for them at the terminal with a polished smile. He was trying to make eye contact with Anu multiple times, which she deliberately avoided. It's been a month since they talked.

Unnatural fatherly affection show-off did not melt kids.

While in car, he was using the mirror to get Anu's attention. He was asking mother about Abu Dhabi days, while father kept quiet. Kids also were not found energetic in presence of Arjun.

As soon as the car stopped in front of her house, Anu got out and walked away to avoid Arjun.

Few weeks of advice from mother and silence of Dad made Anu think of joining a college as lecturer.

The master's degree rank and the national eligibility test lectureship yielded her a job in one of the nearby low profile college.

One year of staying apart and involving with kids and students gave peace in abundance to Anu as never before.

Arjun's parents never tried to make him understand what a partner is. Anu remembered those days she spent at her home with broken right arm which came as a result of assault from Arjun. He never bothered to ask about it as for him she was a golden goose for sex only.

Φ

"Anu, where have you been? I called mom and she told that you just went somewhere without telling anybody anything... what happened to you? Why are you so disturbed? I was so worried and you are not talking to me either..."

She remained silent for few seconds to Arjun's made up care statements over phone. The swift current of memories flashed through her mind and she was not able to talk. She hung up the call and switched off the phone, got inside a cab to go back home.

As the cab was moving fast memories ran down her mind rather fast. She remembered how she has changed from the young girl who loved the world to a woman who feels dejected and depressed by anything and everything around her. So long she had been drifting along the current of life. But now it's time to steer. She can't let the flow sweep away her dreams. She wanted to live, for herself. She had to look after her kids, the priceless possession of her life. She had made it quite clear to herself that unless she fights for herself, her own cause, nothing is happening.

Φ

As Anu joined the job, she felt relieved of many complex emotions which irrupted in her. She started learning to elope with her thoughts into the darkest corners of mind where she creates life as either humans or animals or nature, as relief exercises. As she ascends downhill the emotional creations, sometimes she slips and gets exalted by the time she crosses the state of trance to get conscious. Aadi has been a great support and he taught her to divest herself into the hues of green, nature.

Aadi saw million shades of green when he see what's just green for others - dark green, winsor green, cobalt green, sap green, golden green... everything. The various shades of green were painted with some instantaneous splashes of yellow, red and pinkish purple here and there. The yellowish green of the golden rain tree or cassia with the golden flowers drooping down... the butea or fire in the forest as it is called with the bright red flowers popping up... and the lilac shaded wild champa flowers .... Altogether it appeared as if it was the masterpiece of a great artist.

As the conversations deepened, Anjali and Shivani started getting classes on the different shades and tints of the colour green. They were introduced to Aadi for better clarity on those curious cute little questions.

Anu started waiting for Anju and Shiva asking innocently,

"Amma, can we go to Aadi's place?"

He liked them calling him by name rather than those stereotype 'respectful usages'.

Aadi had a huge collection of nature science videos which Anju and Shiva found interest in watching as they visit Aadi's place.

Just as they were about to leave once, Anu tripped off a step. Aadi who was waiting for the kids caught Anu and in a sudden reflex and pulled her towards him. Anu was tugged on to Aadi's torso and after a blink her eyes locked into his. For few seconds both stood awestruck till Anju came running down to them.

As the kids walked away, Anu turned to Aadi and smiled.

The moon was all set to cast her spell when the kittens with their mother reached back home.

The mermaid was diving to the stream of glittering waters spelt by the moon with stars... the shores were moss clad bottle green in colour and the slimy rocks a much darker shade of the same. Smiling at those little fishes, she swam into the depths of the emerald green river.

CHAPTER VIII

Coincidentally, on Aadi's birthday Anu could convince her parents for permission to visit to a temple near Aadi's house.

It was almost eight in the evening when she started back from the temple. The moon was shining high up there casting the silver beams all over the house, Aadi's house. The sky blue colour walls of the house seemed transmuted with the dark experiences of the people living inside it. The sounds of the crickets were blocked by the sacred hymns from the temple coming through the loud speakers. It's been almost twelve years since she came to the temple. Now the agenda is to show the temple visit to visit her god at his house.

The reason for delay, if anyone asks, can be the visit to Aadi's father who was suffering from Parkinson's disease since long and was bedridden. Aadi's mother, who was a school teacher, knew about the friendship of Anu and Aadi during school ages.

Anu gently opened the gate and entered the courtyard. It was all dark in there apart from the flashes of light coming from the passing vehicles and the moon was trying hard to reach the ground. She stepped in to the house with brisk but twitchy steps.

Anushna climbed the stair and gently opened the door. A single bulb hung from the ceiling with numerous filaments. The salmon colour walls of the room got effused a monochromatic yellow colour with the bulb light.

Aadi, who was reading some book which read its title as VERDICAL, lifted up his head and in a sudden subliminal gesture sprang up. "Anu..." he gasped. "But it's late..."

Anu walked close and held him by his face and holding it tight by his ears she kissed on his lips.

Aadi, taken aback by the sudden act of passion looked her as if he's in a trance. Anu looked at his eyes and smiled. Aadi took her hands and took her to his chamber. Her dominance was seen no more and was soon replaced by a kittenish grin. The cheeks were blushing and she was no longer able to look into his eyes. Aadi, seeing Anu's scarlet lips and bashful expression, held her just above the hips and tugged her towards him...their loins rubbing each other. Anu felt Aadi for the first time. She flinched, and tried to move back, but couldn't. The heat and passion made her feel him and she endured a feeling of elation.

The blue eagle came to the white dove and they both started flying together in circles above the sky... the little girl could see the angel flying right above the eagles and blessing them.... The sky turned azure blue and there was light all over the place. The blue eagle paved way for the dove and both flew away among the stars.

An hour went without notice and Anu stayed relaxed on Aadi's torso, hugging him tight. Aadi fixed his eyes to the farthest corner in his room and dipped himself in deep ponder.

"What happened Aadi? Why? Are you not happy that I..." Anu turned to and sought reason for his silence.

Aadi closed her mouth and made her gulp her words, looking at her eyes. Anushna looked at him not understanding what to say more.

Aadi continued, "We have to wait Anu...till the legal divorce get effected, and we will wait. And then... a whole life before us...doesn't worry... we'll make everything happen..."

Aadi comforted her and caressed her tresses and continued.

"Once legally you and kids are out of this relationship, we don't have to convince anyone around us... No feeling of guilt should be able to devour our happiness."

Her phone rang suddenly telling 'Arjun calling'..!

Anu's pupils shifted from phone screen to Aadi's eyes. Aadi signalled to pick the call.

"I need to talk with you. I shall come to your home with my parents". The serious voice of Arjun not only increased her heartbeat, but dried her throat too.

She did not talk, and he assumed it a 'yes' and hung up.

Aadi did not move but continued to stare at Anu's face. She stood up and turned to the mirror against the bed to put back her hair bun.

She was breathing heavily, as Aadi sat on the bed watching her hurry dressing up.

Anu turned back and walked to him trying to smile. Holding her shoulders with both his arms Aadi told Anu with a sigh.

"Do not worry dear. Tell everything to people and let them understand your pain." Anu looked at him with blank face.

"How do you feel Aadi when someone else, whom you don't love, touches you...? I do not want to go back to that life Aadi."

Aadi put back Anu's dupatta to her and smiled back.

"I know Anu... I know what you are going through right now.... But we need to wait... for our kids... for our life... so that..."

A car in front of Aadi's house honked impatiently.

"It must be Dad. I'll come back Aadi... to this very same place..."

She smiled and continued.

"I may not be able to look at you from there...down the road...So don't come out...bye"

Horn sounded again.

Anu rushed towards the door...turned back ran towards Aadi pulled down the neckline of his black kurta and kissed his bosom...the most passionate kiss so far...leaving the scarlet print of her lips there.

"I'll be back ...love you Aadi... and Happy birthday"

He kept on looking at Anu as she walked away.

As she came down the stairs, she couldn't find anybody out there but heard the clanging vessels and she realized that his mother will be there in the kitchen. She walked to Aadi's mother.

"Aunty, I actually came to the temple and then thought of just dropping by and check"

Thirteen years lives of either side were talked in next few minutes.

Anu met Aadi's dad.

She was looking at him all through the time and finally asked his mother about recovery. She smiled in reply, which never reflected hope.

"Aadi's there... upstairs, reading something" Pointing the stairs to first floor, Aadi's mother replied.

"It's okay Aunty, Dad is waiting in car..." Anu tried to act normal hiding her smile and continued "Just tell him I came. I'm in a hurry actually. Bye Aunty. Take care"

She held Aadi's mother's hand and bid adieu and briskly walked to the gate where her father was waiting in car.

He was asking something to her and then looked at the gate where Aadi's mother walked down, but Anu was deafened by a mixture of thoughts.

Trying hard to hide a smile, she got inside the car, not giving face to Dad.

Car started and Anu, fixing head straight to the bonnet, her eyes wandered in the balcony where Aadi was standing holding the handrails and silently she spelled 'Bye'.

CHAPTER IX

"Let's revert to the point where we start again and again... reviving the spirit and spice of life..."Aadi's words reverberated inside her ears producing ripples of happiness at back of her head. She was ready. Had her bags packed and all set for the journey... a journey of her life...

It was when Aadi gave a talk on 'Time travel' to the students of Anu's college, during the 'Space week' celebrations.

It was already October and the faculties in charge of science club were running the corners to find a speaker.

Anu walked in late for the meeting that planned to announce a regret notice for not having a speaker that year. She suggested Aadityan, the Physicist. And at once, it was accepted.

"Those kids loved it, they're asking for some other topic also from same speaker"

Anu smiled and told Aadi with pride, as she got into his car.

"They were awesome. I loved those questions from them"

Aadi acknowledged as he shifted gear.

The small girl of almost eight is playing on the top of a rocky mount, covered on all sides by lush greenery. The various hues of green are making the scene so lively and energetic. She sees the white headed brahminy kite moving around in circles around her head. She calls out "angel's eagle" and wishes to be with the eagle up above in the sky making circles in the air flying freely above all the obstacles. She slowly found two wings growing on both sides of her

body slowly fluttering them slowly lifted her upwards. In a moment she was among the clouds which floated around her and she is winging her way up to the sun... the warmth of a fatherly affection.

Φ

"Close your eyes Aadi... and don't open till I ask you..." She said.

Aadi closed his eyes but could feel Anu moving towards him. He wondered what she was up to now.

"Now open" her stern voice made him open his eyes and he saw Anu standing there in front of Aadi, both facing the mirror in the cupboard in his room.

Aadi's parents stayed at the physician's clinic for his Dad's treatment which continued for a week. Anu came home with Aadi after the lecture at college.

As they both stood looking at each other in the mirror, he came close to her and rested his face on her shoulder as she smiled and took his palms and kissed. Aadi staring at her eyes, kissed on her neck. Her coyness elated his hormones and his hands moved down towards her pelvis. His hands went through the white Bengal cotton sari and touched her belly. The fingers crept along the sides coming towards the front and touched her navel. Anu closed her eyes in ecstasy. Aadi slowly came forward and sat on his knees, slightly pulled off her sari and gently kissed her belly button. His tongue searched the salty sweat from inside the deep navel. Unable to hold on Anu grabbed Aadi's hands, her body stiffened and it arrested her from moving. Aadi looked at her eyes as she caressed his beard with a smile.

The small girl stood below the raised platform of the stage. Teachers called out names and groups randomly. Five boys and a girl climbed up the stage with the percussion

instruments and sat in a row. The little girl saw the boy sitting in the front, one of her height wearing a charming smile. The peach coloured t-shirt added to the fair looks more clearly and the black thread in his neck with a golden amulet in it made him appear a virtuous boy. She got transfixed on him. The Mrudangam sounded like a dulcet rumbling of thunder and she felt like dancing like a peacock in the splash of summer rain that was trying to sooth her.

Φ

Lying in his arms, she asked.

"Can I give birth to your dreams?"

For this..., Aadi did not reply but smiled and winked at her.

CHAPTER X

The phone in passenger sear lit up with the 6.00 AM alarm. Anu did snooze it by swiping. No messages yet.

Anu watched the raindrops flowing down the windscreen of her car and she felt it was her worries being swept away like that. Even while preoccupied by the non-responsiveness from Aadi, thought of being loved the way she wants brought smile to Anu's lips.

Φ

It was one of the most beautiful days of her life. She was overwhelming with joy as Aadi drove the car through the highway. She was imbibing a new sense of being loved the way she always craved for. She expected the rain to never cease from her path of joy. She again closed her eyes in order to feel the bliss of love.

Suddenly she opened eyes, as she remembered that the otherwise regular periods has not arrived for the current month. But its quiet unlikely as even after both deliveries she had an unusually regular menstruation period.

"What?" Aadi got curious seeing Anu waking up from a trance to some reality thoughts.

"Nothing..." She smiled again and reassured holding Aadi's left hand which was on gear shaft.

As soon as Aadi dropped Anu at her place, she took out phone and sent a message to her Obstetrician, seeking her availability for a phone call.

Anxiety filled the air in and around Anu. She was acting mechanically to those at home in response to their questions.

"Now" She saw the phone screen lit with a reply message from her doctor.

Anu went to room closing the door behind and phoned her. Listening to Anu, doctor advised to wait for few more days and do a pregnancy test. When Anu reminded of the surgical contraception done after birth of Anjali, doctor replied that rarely it is reversible naturally at times.

Anu was experiencing a mixture of emotions on hanging up the call, as she felt the heaviness of balancing the anxiety of answering parents, relatives and the kids on one side and the happiness of the bondage with Aadi on the other side.

A message from Arjun appeared on this.

"I know about the relationship you have with Aadityan. I would never let you live peacefully with him. If I'm not having you, I would never let anyone else have you. Ask him to start counting his days. Not different for you also, either you remain my slave or die."

Anu held her breath for few seconds not knowing what to respond, but she decided not to reply.

The evening was cloudy due to some pressure dip in Bay of Bengal and heavy rain prediction. Anu also felt dark rain clouds maundering in her brain. She felt disconnected, but responded unusually peaceful to her mother's prattling.

Anu scrolled up the messages in phone reading through those threatening ones from Arjun, consoling ones from her doctor, and advices on legal sides of divorce from her lawyer, love and care messages from Aadi.

She sent "take care, be safe for us" to Aadi's phone as message.

CHAPTER XI

Anu tapped the phone screen to discover that it was 6.10 AM as the day light started fanning out from the east. The thought of the left out distance to Aadi's place made her press the accelerator pedal deep down.

A speeding car against her on the other lane of road brushed her rear view mirror and went past, which shook her and left chillness down her spine.

Her mind went blank for a moment. Gasping heavily, she slowed down the car and stopped by the side of the road.

It was a catapult of mind for an instant from those continuous thoughts about Aadi, kids, parents, Arjun and many, but it did not last long.

Anu took phone and dialled her father.

"Anu dear... drive safe keeping away all worries. Anything can be sorted out!" Father responded on one ring itself.

"I'm sorry daddy. I know I'm not a good woman. But please try to understand I have been honestly trying to accept and move on"

On a pause, she felt only silence as response from other side for this. Anu was not surprised though.

"I have only obeyed everyone around me. Never did I demand or fought for my wishes so far. All that done to me with labels of 'For good' has been accepted without any resistance so far. Now, after eight years of marriage, I am left with no other choice but to escape from Arjun for saving myself and my kids"

Anu wiped her eyes and looked far away in silence.

"I know you guys gave him silent approval for branding me mentally ill by taking to his friend psychologist. I do not know whether the loudness of a scream only would wake you up. I'm tired of this toxic life and I hope I will find relief in leaving and living for my kids"

She wept on finishing. It is then her dad broke his silence.

"Anu, I know Aadityan is a good man".

He continued after a pause.

"Father is the one who protects the children; Husband is the one who lives for his wife. I understand Arjun was never both. If you believe Aadityan can be one, we will stand by you. I know it is late, but be assured that your parents are with you on this. Go to him and call and tell us he's safe"

She heard her mom weeping behind with words chorus to those of dad. Anu's tears rolled down her cheeks and this time it is out of shear happiness on knowing she's having her father by her. She cried like a little kid.

"Thank you daddy!. That means a lot to a weak girl like me"

"No you're not weak. It's hard to survive for eight years alone, growing two girls. You're strong my dear. Come home safe, with your man"

Anu felt the mirage of life slowly turning into a real oasis. She cried again on hanging up.

Still no message from Aadi and Anu felt the heaviness somewhere between nose and throat. A pain in her gluteal muscle made her stretch her right leg away from the pedals. With great relief from parents' side, Anu started again to make sure her man is safe.

As soon as she entered the lane, she felt her phone ringing again. As Anu stretched to pick the phone with seat belt on, her foot accidentally pressed the accelerator and the car crossed the median line. Suddenly she realized it and caught hold of the steering wheel to control the vehicle but another speeding car almost reached right in front of her. She had to turn the steering to left hard to avoid head on collision. The other car driver also tried his best to divert it to his left.

Her car hit the right corner of the heading car bonnet causing it to topple and roll into the shrubs by the road side.

Her car made few circles, skidding on road before stopping. The loud noise of the hit, skid and that of shattering of glass made many other vehicles stop by at a few distance away.

People are rushing calling out loudly in panic "Accident!" A huge jolt shook the road and died slowly into silence with time. It was less crowded though.

Anu, despite having seat belt, hit her head on the windscreen and the air bag deflated slowly to make her lean on to the steering wheel. Blood was dripping from Anu's face on to her lap, numbness spread all over the body and she was not able to move her limbs.

The right side of the other car was crushed on the impact and the roll.

It looked as if it's difficult for anyone to survive such a blow. People who ran near attempted to pull the driver of the toppled car out. They had to break the front right door and a portion of the front glass to pull him out. Blood was gushing out of many places from his body and head. His white t-shirt became blood red by the time he was pulled out.

He's a middle aged man with beard and broken spectacles.

The phone in his car was showing a connecting call.

"Calling Anushna..."

By then two ambulances rushed to the spot. Anu was pulled out through the windscreen and was carried to one of the ambulance in a stretcher. Pain has numbed her body and blood flowing down her forehead blinding everything around. All the noise around has faded as her ears were still ringing much loudly and unpleasantly.

As they moved her to the ambulance, she saw a familiar face, 'Aadi', wearing a blood tinted white t-shirt and lying half way out of the windscreen.

He's drenched in blood and was felt helpless. His face was painted red with blood, arms hung down seemingly boneless as they lifted him out of the car. His white t-shirt has blood strokes with different intensities. Blood drips from his body while people make him lie down on the road. Someone was shaking him and trying to wake him up. Aadi turns his face in pain and Anu sees him looking at her.

Blood from her eyebrows makes everything blurred, but she's unable to wipe them.

Anu wanted to scream in the loudest possible voice, knowing that she hit Aadi's car and the nightmare has come real paradoxically. She was losing her consciousness in pain, both of mind and body.

Epilogue

Aadi's palms held her firm and snug as if he's calming her.

She knew it is unreal.

She knew he's gone, forever.

And she knew this is nothing more than her mind fobbing her own self.

Horrendous moments squeezed her heart, while her mind told Aadi sitting besides, smiling at her.

It's the 'dungeon' smile.

Anu closed her eyes slowly as the tear mixed with blood stream from her nose, dripped on to the floor. Drenched in blood, her glinting diamond nose pin had stories to tell.

She's falling slowly into the semblance of a painless slumber.

Anu was shook by one of the attender inside the ambulance, as letting her go unconscious is dangerous.

Eyes closed, but she was breathing.

Φ

Anu could clearly see the happenings of previous day evening, when her phone lit up saying 'Aadi calling...' in a least expected moment.

In came the question from his 10 year younger voice than his real age,

"Anu, if free and craving for a walk with your buddy, then come over now. Let me show you a special place!"

It's exactly when she was collecting the blood report from the lab to clarify regarding pregnancy.

It says positive!

That confirms the two lines appeared in the pregnancy confirmation strip.

She's pregnant.., pregnant with Aadi's baby.

The surgical contraception gave way to the 'love' to swim up to 'mate with the craving to live', inside a woman.

Her mind went past galaxies which are light-years away, to a world they've imagined. A parallel world..., where dreams of this world is a reality.

She's excited and equally confused and tensed as she's not divorced legally yet.

What burnt her mind was how to let him know that she's carrying his love in her belly.

In the middle of all these, she acted normal and replied to him.

"Special place?... where's it?"

"You'll know...Come over anyways, I'll show you, meet me at college gate in one hour"

Anu's joy knew no bounds. She got back the most needed smile on her lips after the stressful day fighting with her mom on being sombre about life with Aadi.

"I would love to join Mr. Buddy, but let me check with Mom, as she was asking me to leave for buying groceries. And, should I bring kiddos?, they have many million questions for you about sun, moon, oceans and many".

Aadi took a pause before replying "That'll be cool!"

The intonation of his voice silently conveyed that he wanted some private time with her alone and since she asked, he couldn't say no regarding kiddos. Understanding it, she replied him in the same warmth.

"Else we both meet this time; kiddos can have a separate session!"

And in no time came the excited 'Yes' from Aadi.

"So if I can get out all by myself, we may go for a walk and will see the special place you want me to see. But Aadi, I need to come back not too late as I'm dropping Shivani for her dance classes on my way"

Anu paused a bit and continued.

"Aadi... I have something to tell you."

But Aadi has already hung up, excited and walked to take the keys of his car to start off.

After about one hour, he received a call from Anu, "Buddy, where are you? I'm waiting outside the campus main gate."

It was the same college where Aadi graduated from, which is famous for the lush green campus, 'nesting place for birds of different flocks'.

"Okay, walk straight past the main entrance and enter the small gate, come over there", said Aadi.

"The post office gate!?"

Anu knew the small gate as she's seen it as she passed by it a couple of times while taking shortcut to reach her maternal house. She walked swiftly but with anxious thoughts about the 'special place', and thoughts about the special news to Aadi.

The flight of steps from the gate leads to a post office in the campus.

The depleted plaster on the walls made it look antique. The creepers hung those from the tiled roof reminded of Shivani's curls falling to her forehead. There were wood logs aesthetically placed to arrange a sitting area.

As she was climbing those mud clad steps, she saw Aadi standing there scrolling mobile phone, leaning on to the short badam tree, wearing an off white shorts and the blue t-shirt. The t-shirt read 'aeonian' written in white lean Gothic font.

Anu remembered reading "the aeonian themes of love and revenge" somewhere in her degree reference books and smiled.

Anu felt some cool air pocket rising through her gullet which appeared as a sigh of relief on meeting Aadi, as she always feels.

She smiled and winked at him.

The confusion on how to reveal the special secret to Aadi was evident from her face.

"Everything all right Anu...?"

Aadi tried to reassure.

Not looking at his eyes, she replied. "Yes" and a pause then again with firmness "Yes..!"

They started walking through the main central road in the campus where many couples walked past them. Aadi talked about the campus and the memories it holds. His words had a lot of life and energy in it. Anu followed him nodding to his words, but her mind was repeatedly chanting the blood report saying 'positive'. It's not the first pregnancy of course, but this time not from husband, while still not divorced. Mixed emotions flashed her mind criss-cross, even while she's sharing air with one who cares for her better than any other person.

"Are you with me Anu..?"

Aadi's voice pulled her back from deeper thoughts.

She smiled and leaned to his arm while walking and reassured him about her complete availability for him.

The beauty in Aadi's explanations is about those minute details which he observes and many others don't even bother to look at. She enjoys listening to him.

They entered a less illuminated long corridor with class rooms on either side. Few students were found walking against them in the corridor.

"KALAPANI!!, that's what we used to call this building while in here. This was my final year classroom"

Aadi smile and pushed open a classroom door. A small organised lecture hall with many inspiring words stuck on one of the walls. One of the walls had a dark green writing board and other had a lot of windows. An overhead screen projector was hung from the roof with few colourful decorative papers dangling from it. Aadi sat on the front row as Anu walked to the windows and got view of the badminton court and the open-air there from there. Aadi joined her at the window, and the badminton court seemed to have brought a trickle of memories in Aadi, as she found him smiling looking at it.

Some applauding noise could be heard from an adjacent lecture hall, and it felt like conclusion of some seminar.

"Okay come" Aadi directed her out of the classroom and they walked towards a less lit stairway. He held her hands and led the way downstairs.

"Where are we going?" Anu felt curious as she held his cold palm tight, with pounding heart.

Turning towards her and gently smiling, Aadi continued to walk. The flight of steps led them to a small platform which further led to another set of stairs. The evening sun has painted boxes on the landing and the stair as sunlight riddled through the grates on the wall. As they almost neared the end of the stairs, Aadi stopped and looked at Anu.

"Anu..., keep your eyes closed, and don't open until I ask you to"

The dusty place was full of cob webs and discarded parts of various machines. Though the wait for the suspense was throbbing in her head, her heart was full of the news which she wants to tell Aadi. Breathing heavily,

Anu kept closed her eyes patiently. Aadi comforted her and walked around taking a quick peep inside the old classroom at the end of the dusty corridor. It felt he was making sure that nobody was around; he came back with two small boxes in hand. He took out a lean candle from his left pocket and lit it with left hand. Opened the bigger box and carefully took out a blackish brown pastry cake. Pressing the candle on to the cake, Aadi hid the small box in his pocket.

"Aadi..." Anu felt discomfort standing alone and blinded from the happenings.

Aadi kept doing his work with his pupils at Anu and smiling.

"Now" Aadi's sound resonated through the corridor and Anu slowly opened her eyes.

The grubby corridor now seemed as if it is a scene from some romantic movie. The golden yellow light from a candle got added on to the amorous ambience of the passage. Aadi stood there at the bottom of the stairs both hands extended, welcoming her. Anu couldn't hold back herself and she ran down the flight of stairs and sprang on to Aadi hugging him tight, immersing her face to his chest.

"Happy Birthday Lavender girl" Aadi whispered in her ears.

Anu couldn't control the tiny droplets of happiness which rolled down from eyes wetting her cheeks.

It was her birthday, and he remembered it. A flash of mixed emotions ran through her head, as she remembered that even her mother did not wish her on this day. Only Shiva and Anju came hugging as they woke up gifting a small greeting card drawn by them saying 'Happy birthday Amma... keep smiling'. The card had the picture of a mother and her two kids on either side holding her arm and walking.

And now in this dungeon, the love of her life has given such a surprise. She remembered that Arjun has never taken any such effort ever since married. It's not about the luxury of ambiance, but the love and care as part of togetherness and the want for each other that matters for a women. Aadi prioritizes those small things over formalities.

"Here, blow the candle... sorry couldn't get a fancy one..." he felt tittering.

"Idiot, this is the best ever surprise in past many years" Anu wiped off her tears in smile and said.

She walked to the cake and blew the candle and took the small spoon by the side of it to cut the birthday cake. The chocolate pastry seemed much tastier than it appeared while she was sharing it with him.

Anu tried to be casual as she was finishing the cake and said, "I am pregnant"

"Wha...What..?" Aadi's eyes stretched wide open.

Anu smiled in peace now.

"Yes, I am carrying.., our baby" She pressed her right hand palm on to underbelly softly as her eyes moved from Aadi's eyes to her belly.

Aadi's expression transformed from surprise to delight and he touched her underbelly over her palm.

The sudden thought of her still valid marriage made him anxious again.

Reading his mind, Anu touched his cheek to ease him through the thoughts.

"A woman needs someone who cares for her smallest feelings, not the one who thinks she's a slave. For Arjun and family, I'm a slave since the day we're married"

After a pause, she continued.

"It is affecting my children too, as they're growing up hating the person whom they're forced to call father. He's not signing the divorce papers as he doesn't want the world to know about the torture he gives."

Pinning her eyes on to Aadi's, she paused for a while. Aadi sighs and continue to hold her palm, nodding head.

Tears rolled down her cheeks as she continued.

"But this news will force him to get away, as I'll be known as a bad woman who indulged with another man, while in a marriage. It's fine for me as mental peace is important than the name which society calls me".

Aadi broke silence.

"Relax Anu; I understand the toxicity of such a relationship, not only to you but for 'our' kids too. I'll stand by and we will be together happily with Anjali, Shivani and...'this guy'. It's a promise".

He kept his palm on her underbelly when both looked down and smiled together as if they see the foetus.

The usage 'Our kids' made Anu smile again and gave an assurance of a proper life by definition.

Aadi continued to smile. He looked more handsome and with an aura around him.

"And a small gift for the happy news..." Aadi took out the small box which he slid into his pocket earlier.

It read the name 'BHIMA jewellery' on top of the box and as Anu opened, she found a shining nose-pin inside.

"Diamond??!!, you remembered it...?!!!"

A moment of silence in surprise, and then watery eyes.

This was a promise made by Aadi on a walk back home after Mr. Vinay's class during those fantasy days of teenage.

Tears of joy replaced that of pain and it exuded down her cheeks as her smile reappeared. She immediately removed her gold nose-pin and replaced it with the diamond stud. All these in the same fixed smile. She did not look at Aadi's face as she was overjoyed with the surprise.

Aadi was gazing at her all these time with amazement. It seemed as if the shimmer in her eyes had grown much bigger and she was becoming more and more beautiful. The dingy corridor was seen no more. They were among the clouds, high up in the sky, feeling weightlessness of some unknown feeling.

Aadi slowly held Anu's face with both his palms, holding underneath her ears. He could feel the pulse on her neck and the thrust gained pace with proximity. She looked into his eyes, where she could see herself.

Aadi leaned to her and softly kissed her temples.

Anu blushed!

Her eyes lolled down and a smile flashed in her lips. As he continued with her temple, she felt his neck, the sweat rolling down touched her lips and she tasted it, salt, and she repeated it a number of times from one end to the other relishing the flavour of her man.

The curious looks in Aadi's eyes were substituted with a kind of dominance mixed with passion and Anu could see the care for her in them.

Aadi hauled her towards his torso and gave her a smooch.

Anu closed her eyes involuntarily; feeling helpless happily and thawed her into him gradually.

Slowly their lips exchanged the love and warmth. Anu's lower one between Aadi's and slowly caressing both with his tongue. He moved from lips to forehead, and then to eyes, ears, cheeks and neck, which melted Anu.

Sighs of pleasure, forgetting what and where they're continued.

“Love you, my lavender girl” Aadi whispered on to her ears in between the kiss.

The girl was nowhere then. He could only smell the fragrance of dreams and desire held for years. The air redolent with the fumes of Anu and Aadi blew across the grime spread in the dungeon, waking up the doggoned souls from the dust.

The two were awakened from the trance with a loud bang they heard from the entrance door soon followed by the clanging of a metal chain. Still in becharm of love, both of them rushed upstairs, but it was late.

Everyone left from the building, locking them inside. Aadi tried pulling the door and the lock chain. A sudden departure of emotions from an ecstatic state to disquietude. Anu was in the verge of breaking down.

After a pause, Aadi smiled and walked pulling Anu down the dungeon, towards the other side of the same corridor. She walked anxiously, as he reached a sliding metal door locked from inside. Breaking the lock with a heavy metal piece they managed to get out of the dungeon.

“KISSPEDITIONS !” looking at those red flowers fallen on the pathway from trees on either side, Aadi said with a smile.

“What?” Anu turned to Aadi’s face with curiosity hearing the new terminology.

He turned to her, smiled and whispered.

“Kiss expeditions... Kisspeditions!”

“Kisspeditions” Anu repeated after him and she couldn’t hold back her laughter. They both laughed in pure happiness, which reverberated in the hazy campus. It was 6.45 PM as Anu looked at her watch.

Holding hands, they both walked through the red and yellow flowers on the pathway, when a breeze went past them fluttering Anu's dupatta.

As she looked up, a wispy rainbow could be seen in sky through the thick green branches of the trees.

9 798887 729398

Printed by Libri Plureos GmbH in Hamburg, Germany